The Glambulance

'The Glambulance'
An original concept by Alison Donald
© Alison Donald

Illustrated by Beth Hughes

Published by MAVERICK ARTS PUBLISHING LTD
Studio 11, City Business Centre, 6 Brighton Road,
Horsham, West Sussex, RH13 5BB
© Maverick Arts Publishing Limited February 2021
+44 (0)1403 256941

A CIP catalogue record for this book is available at the British Library.

ISBN 978-1-84886-769-7

www.maverickbooks.co.uk

Gold

This book is rated as: Gold Band (Guided Reading)

The Glambulance

By **Alison Donald**

Illustrated by **Beth Hughes**

Chapter 1

The Glambulance sped through town with its lights flashing.

"Move out of the way, people, this is a fashion emergency!" Seb, the driver, cried out of the window.

The Glambulance had an unusual mission: to respond to doggy fashion emergencies!

Riding in the Glambulance were two very important dogs:

Pickles, a Beagle who was an expert in dog grooming, and Rosa, a small Pekinese, who was an expert in clipping claws.

Today, they were on their way to help a Pug get ready for an important show.

"Ruff, ruff!" barked Pickles.

"Yap, yap!" shrieked Rosa.

They wanted the cars to get out of their way.

Pickles and Rosa felt the van stop. Seb opened the door for them. "Go work your magic! I'll see what our next emergency is!" He grinned.

The dogs raced out of the Glambulance and towards the dog show.

"There's the Pug," said Pickles.

"Oh my!" said Rosa.

The Pug was brown with mud on one side and also had a broken claw.

"Thank goodness you're here!" cried the owner. "My precious Pug tripped over and he's up for judging soon. Please help!"

Chapter 2

Pickles and Rosa worked fast.

Rosa attached a false claw, then she trimmed and painted all of them.

Pickles washed and dried the Pug. Then he added some glitter spray to the Pug's fur.

"Thanks Pickles and Rosa. You really saved the day!" said the Pug's owner.

Pickles and Rosa wagged their tails to say goodbye, then ran back to the van.

They hopped in and waited for Seb to start the engine, but instead there was a **KNOCK KNOCK** on the window.

"Police," a voice said, "please open the window." Seb jumped and opened the window. "Excuse me, sir, but we would like to question you at the police station. A bank was robbed across the street and we would like to know if you saw anything," said the officer.

Pickles and Rosa stared at each other in surprise.

"What about my dogs?" asked Seb. "I can't leave them all alone."

"They can stay at the dog pound until we're finished."

Pickles and Rosa whimpered. Even if it was temporary, Pickles and Rosa did *not* want to go to the dog pound.

Chapter 3

The dog pound was noisy and smelled damp. Pickles and Rosa were greeted by a friendly lady who smelled like perfume.

"Hello Pickles and Rosa, I'm Grace." She stroked the dogs. "I'll be looking after you today!" She led the dogs to a cage and gave them food, water and tummy rubs. Then they heard a **CLINK** as she closed the door.

Rosa looked around at the rows of cages. "Thank goodness we are only here for the day," she said.

"The hair on some of these dogs is shocking!" said Pickles.

"I know! And just look at the state of their nails!" Rosa tutted.

"And don't get me started on the smell in here!" added Pickles. He looked up, and saw a huge Mastiff who was listening in on their conversation.

"Well, well. Two fancy new dogs who have never been in the pound," the Mastiff chuckled. "Nice to meet you, Pickles and Rosa. You can call me Wrinkles."

Pickles hung his head with embarrassment and Rosa's tail went between her legs.

"Sorry, Wrinkles," said Rosa. "It's just that we're a little nervous being here for the day."

"Well, you're very lucky to only be here for one day. Some of us have been in here for months, even years," Wrinkles said.

"I thought the dogs here got adopted," said Pickles.

"Some do," Wrinkles replied. "Today is an adoption day. We have two adoption hours.

People will come this morning and afternoon, and hopefully some lucky dogs might find an owner."

"How exciting!" said Rosa.

"Just wait and see..." Wrinkles sighed.
He sounded tired.

Chapter 4

Pickles and Rosa watched as Grace opened the door.

A stream of people rushed in, but all of them went straight to Pickles and Rosa's cage. They didn't even bother to look at the other dogs.

"These two look so lovely!" a lady commented

"Sorry, they're only staying for the day,"
Grace explained.

"Oh, what a shame," the lady said.

After a while, all of the visitors left.

"Wait, no one got adopted?" asked Pickles.

"Nope, same as usual," said Wrinkles. "Only the cute ones like you get adopted."

"That's awful!" Rosa whined.

Pickles and Rosa knew that Seb would come back for them, but what about these other dogs?

"Maybe we can help," said Pickles. "We do doggy makeovers every day. Let's give some dogs a tidy-up before the next adoption hour!"

Wrinkles's ears went up. "I can help you," he said. "My old owner was a hairdresser. I spent hours in the shop, watching her style hair."

"Ok," said Rosa. "Let's do this!"

When Grace stepped out for her lunch,
Wrinkles nudged open the cage doors.
He guided Pickles, Rosa, and two other dogs
to the bathroom for their makeovers.

First up was Dot,
who claimed she
was a Dalmatian,
but her coat was
all black.

Pickles used the sink and hand soap to scrub
her clean until she was white with black
spots. Wrinkles found a curtain tie and tied
it in a bow on her head.

Then, Rosa painted her nails with red marker.

"Now you look like a proper Dalmatian again!" cried Rosa.

"I hope I'll get adopted now!" Dot smiled and wagged her tail.

Then, there was a Cockapoo named Sadie.

Her fur was limp, so Wrinkles tied it around some rags and stood her under the hand dryer. When he took the rags out, her fur had loopy curls again. Finally, Wrinkles added some pink bows.

Pickles and Rosa were amazed: Wrinkles was so good at styling hair!

"Thank you so much!" cried Sadie.

Suddenly, they heard Grace coming. The dogs rushed back to their cages just in time. Grace opened the door with a lot of people walking behind her.

Another adoption hour had begun.

Chapter 5

Within ten minutes, Dot and Sadie were both adopted. The dogs barked in celebration.

"Great job!" said Wrinkles.

"You too," woofed Pickles.

"We make a great team!" yapped Rosa.

Pickles and Rosa felt relieved, but they wanted to help more dogs. They had a warm feeling inside seeing these dogs find their forever homes.

Just then, Seb walked through the door.

Pickles and Rosa barked with joy.

"Hello you two! I hope you've been good."
Seb waved, then he turned his attention to
Grace to explain that he was here to collect
them.

"So, I guess you two are leaving now," said
Wrinkles.

"You should come with us," said Rosa.

"That's right, we need you on our
Glambulance team!" Pickles added.

Seb headed over and stroked them.

"I see you made a friend! Come on, we have to help a poodle with an emergency on her wedding day!"

Wrinkles's ears drooped. He would be sad to see Pickles and Rosa go... But just then, Pickles and Rosa stood by his side and barked. They didn't want to leave without him.

"Poor old Wrinkles, he never gets adopted," Grace came over. "He seemed so happy with Pickles and Rosa..."

Seb smiled at her, "Ah well, I can't just leave him then! Maybe he can help Pickles and Rosa with makeovers."

Wrinkles wagged his tail with excitement. Pickles and Rosa barked happily.

Grace was thrilled. "Would you be able to visit again some time? I'd love for your Glambulance team to do makeovers on the dogs here, to help them get adopted," she said.

"That's a lovely idea," Seb agreed. "What do you three think?" he looked at Pickles, Rosa and Wrinkles.

They all barked and wagged their tails. They loved being a part of the Glambulance, and they couldn't wait to help all the other dogs find their forever homes too.

The End

Book Bands for Guided Reading

The Institute of Education book banding system is a scale of colours that reflects the various levels of reading difficulty. The bands are assigned by taking into account the content, the language style, the layout and phonics. Word, phrase and sentence level work is also taken into consideration.

Maverick Early Readers are a bright, attractive range of books covering the pink to white bands. All of these books have been book banded for guided reading to the industry standard and edited by a leading educational consultant.

To view the whole Maverick Readers scheme, visit our website at www.maverickearlyreaders.com

Or scan the QR code above to view our scheme instantly!